TOOLS FOR CAREGIVERS

- **ATOS:** 0.7
- **GRL:** C
- **WORD COUNT:** 30

- **CURRICULUM CONNECTIONS:** animals, habitats

Skills to Teach

- **HIGH-FREQUENCY WORDS:** cannot, mom, see, she, the, them, they
- **CONTENT WORDS:** carries, cleans, cubs, grow, helps, look, new, nurses, play, teaches, tiger, up, yet
- **PUNCTUATION:** exclamation points, periods
- **WORD STUDY:** long /a/, spelled ay (play); long /e/, spelled ea (cleans, teaches); long /e/, spelled ee (see); long /o/, spelled ow (grow); multisyllable words (baby, carries, nurses, teaches)
- **TEXT TYPE:** information report

Before Reading Activities

- Read the title and give a simple statement of the main idea.
- Have students "walk" though the book and talk about what they see in the pictures.
- Introduce new vocabulary by having students predict the first letter and locate the word in the text.
- Discuss any unfamiliar concepts that are in the text.

After Reading Activities

The text explains how tiger mothers and cubs interact. A tiger mother cares for her cubs. How does this compare to how the readers' caregivers care for them? Ask the readers if they have siblings. Are there any ways they interact with their families that mirror how tiger families interact? Ask them to explain their answers.

Tadpole Books are published by Jump!, 5357 Penn Avenue South, Minneapolis, MN 55419, www.jumplibrary.com

Copyright ©2019 Jump. International copyright reserved in all countries. No part of this book may be reproduced in any form without written permission from the publisher.

Editor: Jenna Trnka **Designer:** Anna Peterson

Photo Credits: GlobalP/iStock, cover, 1; Anan Kaewkhammul/Shutterstock, 2–3, 16tr; Dennis Jacobsen/Shutterstock, 4–5, 16tl; Tom Brakefield/Getty, 6–7, 16bl; noise-fotografie/Photocase, 8–9, 16tm; Gary Vestal/Getty, 10–11, 16br; moosehenderson/Shutterstock, 12–13, 16bm; Abhishek Singh/Dreamstime, 14–15.

Library of Congress Cataloging-in-Publication Data
Names: Nilsen, Genevieve, author.
Title: Tiger cubs / by Genevieve Nilsen.
Description: Tadpole edition. | Minneapolis, MN : Jump!, Inc., (2019) | Series: Safari babies | Includes index.
Identifiers: LCCN 2018024756 (print) | LCCN 2018027525 (ebook) | ISBN 9781641282482 (ebook) | ISBN 9781641282468 (hardcover : alk. paper) | ISBN 9781641282475 (paperback)
Subjects: LCSH: Tiger—Infancy—Juvenile literature.
Classification: LCC QL737.C23 (ebook) | LCC QL737.C23 N564 2019 (print) | DDC 599.75613/92—dc23
LC record available at https://lccn.loc.gov/2018024756

SAFARI BABIES

TIGER CUBS

by Genevieve Nilsen

TABLE OF CONTENTS

TIGER CUBS

Look! New tiger cubs.

cub

They cannot see yet.

mom

Mom helps.

She carries them.

She nurses them.

She cleans them.

She teaches them.

The cubs play.

They grow up!

WORDS TO KNOW

carries

cleans

cubs

nurses

play

teaches

INDEX